JON AGEE
MILO'S HAT TRICK

P9-APY-249

 DIAL BOOKS FOR YOUNG READERS

For Audrey

Dial Books for Young Readers
Penguin Young Readers Group
An imprint of Penguin Random House LLC
375 Hudson Street, New York, NY 10014

Copyright © 2001, 2017 by Jon Agee

Originally published by Hyperion Book for Children.
This edition with several new illustrations is published by Dial Books for Young Readers.

Penguin supports copyright. Copyright fuels creativity, encourages diverse voices, promotes free speech, and creates a vibrant culture. Thank you for buying an authorized edition of this book and for complying with copyright laws by not reproducing, scanning, or distributing any part of it in any form without permission. You are supporting writers and allowing Penguin to continue to publish books for every reader.

Printed in China
ISBN 9780735229877

1 3 5 7 9 10 8 6 4 2

Design by Lily Malcom
Text set in Corona

He was called Milo the Magnificent. But Milo wasn't magnificent at all. He botched his card trick. He tangled his rope trick. And his hat trick was just pathetic.

Mr. Popovich, the theater manager, was furious. "Milo!" he barked. "I'll give you one more chance. Tomorrow night you better pull a rabbit out of your hat—or else."

So the next morning, Milo went out to catch a rabbit.

Instead, he caught a bear.

"What are you doing out here?" said the bear.

"Uh, I'm looking for a rabbit . . . for my hat trick."

"Hat trick?" said the bear. "Maybe I can help."

"You?" said Milo.

"Watch this," said the bear.

And he jumped into Milo's hat.

"Wow!" said Milo. "How did you do that?"

"Easy," said the bear. "You just pretend your bones are
made of rubber. It's a secret I learned from a rabbit."

"You definitely can help me out," said Milo. "But you'll
have to hide in my hat until we're on stage."

"No problem," said the bear. "Just whistle and I'll pop out."

On the train back to the city, Milo was in a daze. "It's true!" he thought. "I really do have a bear in my hat!" But when he got to his dressing room, his hat was empty. Worse yet—it wasn't even his hat!

Milo raced back to the train station. There were lots of people with hats, but none of the hats was his.

Meanwhile, in a restaurant across town, someone whistled for a waiter.

"TA-DA!"
Right on cue, the bear popped out
of the hat. But there was no applause.
There was no Milo!
"Uh-oh," said the bear.
He grabbed Milo's hat and ran.

"Help!" cried a cabdriver. "A wild bear is on the loose!"

"A bear? Where?" said a policeman.

"He was standing right by that mailbox. Then—poof!— he disappeared."

"Oh, gosh!" said the bear. "How in the world will I ever find that magician?"

Just then a schoolteacher was passing the mailbox. "Hurry up, children!" she said. "Or we'll be late for the magic show!"

"Magic show?" thought the bear. He slipped out of the mail slot and quickly joined the line.

Minutes before the matinee, Milo slouched into the theater. "It's no use, Mr. Popovich," he said. "I didn't find a rabbit."

"Rabbit or no rabbit, you've got to go on," Mr. Popovich said. "Just look, the house is packed!"

Milo looked. A very familiar hat was sitting in the front row.

"My hat! Would you please hand me my hat?"

Milo whistled and out popped the bear.
"Boy," said the bear, "am I glad to see you!"

For the rest of the afternoon, the bear jumped in
and out of hats of all shapes and sizes.
Milo's new act was a smash!

Mr. Popovich was ecstatic. For three solid weeks,
Milo and the bear were the hottest ticket in town.

But one day, during intermission, the bear yawned
an enormous yawn. After popping in and out of seven
hundred and sixty-two hats, he was pooped.

So Milo took the bear home.

Back in his cave, the bear settled down for a long nap.

"Gee," said Milo, "what am I going to do without you?"

The bear yawned. "Like I said before, you just . . ."

And then he was asleep.

These days, Milo closes his
show with a hat trick.
And this one is really special.

It's a secret he learned from a bear.